2B

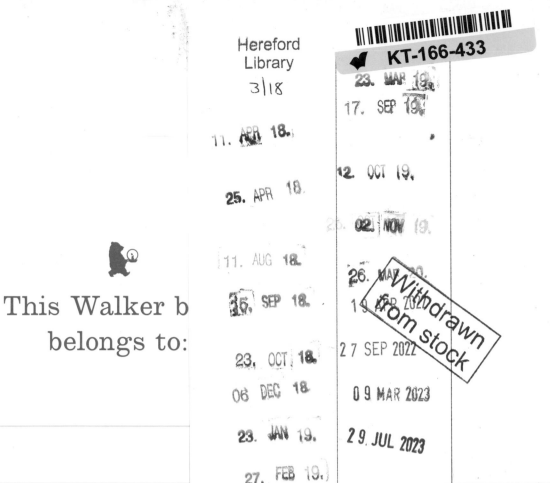

This Walker b

belongs to:

In loving memory of Carol J. Buckley, shining star
of the Cornell Library, who always had room
in her heart for a new friend.
We miss you.

M. K.

To Priscilla, our first personal librarian.

K. H.

First published 2006 by Walker Books Ltd
87 Vauxhall Walk, London SE11 5HJ

This edition published 2008

14 16 18 20 19 17 15

Text © 2006 Michelle Knudsen
Illustrations © 2006 Kevin Hawkes

The right of Michelle Knudsen and Kevin Hawkes to be identified as
author and illustrator respectively of this work has been asserted by
them in accordance with the Copyright, Designs and Patents Act 1988

This book has been typeset in New Clarendon

Printed in China

British Library Cataloguing in Publication Data:
a catalogue record for this book is available from the British Library

ISBN 978-1-4063-0567-8

www.walker.co.uk

Library Lion

MICHELLE KNUDSEN

illustrated by

KEVIN HAWKES

WALKER BOOKS

AND SUBSIDIARIES

LONDON • BOSTON • SYDNEY • AUCKLAND

One day, a lion came to the library.
He walked right past the front desk
and disappeared between the bookshelves.

Mr McBee ran down the hall to the head librarian's office. "Miss Merriweather!" he shouted.

"No running," said Miss Merriweather, without looking up.

"But there's a lion!" said Mr McBee. "In the library!"

"Is he breaking any rules?" asked Miss Merriweather. She was very particular about rule breaking.

"Well, no," said Mr McBee. "Not really."

"Then leave him be."

The lion wandered around the library.
He sniffed the card index.

He rubbed his head against the new book collection.

Then he padded over to the story corner and went to sleep.

No one knew what to do. There weren't any rules about lions in the library.

It was soon storytime. There weren't any rules about lions at storytime either.

The story lady seemed a little nervous. But she read out the title of the first book in a strong, clear voice. The lion looked up. The story lady kept on reading.

The lion stayed for the next story. And the story after that. He waited for another story, but the children began to walk away.

"Storytime is over," a little girl told him.

The lion looked at the children. He looked at the story lady. He looked at the closed books. Then he roared very loudly.

RAAAHHRRRR!

Miss Merriweather came marching out of her office. "Who is making that noise?" she demanded.

"It's the lion," said Mr McBee.

Miss Merriweather marched over to the lion. "If you can't be quiet, then you'll have to leave," she said in a stern voice. "Those are the rules!"

The lion kept roaring. He sounded sad.

The little girl tugged on Miss Merriweather's dress. "If he promises to be quiet, can he come back for storytime tomorrow?" she asked.

The lion stopped roaring. He looked at Miss Merriweather.

Miss Merriweather looked back. Then she said, "Yes. A nice, quiet lion would certainly be allowed to come back for storytime tomorrow."

"Hooray!" cried the children.

The next day, the lion came back.

"You're early," said Miss Merriweather. "Storytime isn't until three o'clock."

The lion did not move.

"Very well," said Miss Merriweather. "You might as well make yourself useful." She sent him off to dust the encyclopaedias until storytime.

The next day, the lion arrived early again.
This time, Miss Merriweather asked him to lick
the envelopes for the overdue notes.

Soon the lion started doing jobs without being asked. He dusted the encyclopaedias. He licked the envelopes. He let small children stand on his back to reach the books on the highest shelves.

Then he curled up in the story corner to wait for storytime to begin.

At first, people in the library were nervous about the lion, but soon they were used to having him there. In fact, he seemed very well suited to the library. His big feet were quiet on the library floor. He made a comfy backrest for the children at storytime. And he never roared in the library any more.

"What a helpful lion," people said. They patted his soft head as he walked by. "How did we ever get by without him?"

Mr McBee scowled when he heard that. They had always managed fine before. No lions were needed! Lions, he thought, could not understand rules. They did not belong in the library.

One day, after he had dusted all the encyclopaedias and licked all the envelopes and helped all the small children, the lion padded down the hall to Miss Merriweather's office to see what else there was to do. There was still a while until storytime.

"Hello, Lion," said Miss Merriweather. "I have something you can do. You can take a book back to the front desk for me. Let me just get it down from the shelf."

Miss Merriweather stepped up onto the stool. The book was just out of her reach.

Miss Merriweather stood on her toes. She stretched out her fingers.

"Almost … there…" she said.

Then Miss Merriweather stretched a little too far.

"Ouch," said Miss Merriweather softly.
She did not get up.

"Mr McBee!" she called after a minute.
"Mr McBee!"

But Mr McBee was at the front desk.
He could not hear her calling.

"Lion," said Miss Merriweather. "Please
go and get Mr McBee."

The lion ran down the hall.

"No running," Miss Merriweather called
after him.

He put his big paws up on the front desk and looked at Mr McBee.

"Go away, Lion," said Mr McBee. "I'm busy."

The lion whined. He pointed his nose down the hall towards Miss Merriweather's office.

Mr McBee ignored him.

Finally, the lion did the only thing he could think of to do. He looked Mr McBee straight in the eye. Then he opened his mouth very wide. And he roared the loudest roar he had ever roared in his life.

Mr McBee gasped.

"You're not being quiet!" he said to the lion. "You're breaking the rules!"

Mr McBee walked down the hall as fast as he could.

The lion did not follow him. He had broken the rules. He knew what that meant. He hung his head and walked towards the door.

Mr McBee did not notice. "Miss Merriweather!" he called as he walked. "Miss Merriweather! The lion has broken the rules! The lion has broken the rules!"

He burst into Miss Merriweather's office.

She was not in her chair.

"Miss Merriweather?" he asked.

"Sometimes," said Miss Merriweather from the floor behind her desk, "there is a good reason to break the rules. Even in the library. Now please go and call a doctor. I think I've broken my arm."

Mr McBee ran to call a doctor.

"No running!" Miss Merriweather called after him.

The next day things were back to normal –
almost.

Miss Merriweather's left arm was in a
sling. The doctor had told her not to work
too hard.

I will have my lion to help me, Miss
Merriweather thought. But the lion did not
come to the library that morning.

At three o'clock, Miss Merriweather
walked over to the story corner. The story
lady was just starting to read. The lion was
not there.

People in the library kept looking up
from their books and computers, hoping
that they would see a familiar furry face.
But the lion did not come that day.

The lion did not come the next day
either. Or the day after that.

One evening, Mr McBee stopped at Miss Merriweather's office as he was leaving the library. "Can I do anything for you before I go, Miss Merriweather?" he asked her.

"No, thank you," said Miss Merriweather. She was looking out of the window. Her voice was very quiet. Even for the library.

Mr McBee frowned as he walked away. He thought there probably was something he could do for Miss Merriweather.

Mr McBee left the library. But he did not go home.

He walked around the nearby streets.
He looked under cars. He looked behind bushes.

He looked in back gardens and rubbish bins and up trees.

Finally he ended up back at the library.

The lion was sitting outside, looking in through the glass doors.

"Hello, Lion," said Mr McBee.

The lion did not turn around.

"I thought you might like to know," said Mr McBee, "that there's a new rule at the library. No roaring allowed, unless you have a very good reason – say, if you're trying to help a friend who's been hurt, for example."

The lion's ears twitched. He turned around. But Mr McBee was already walking away.

The next day, Mr McBee walked down the hall to Miss Merriweather's office.

"What is it, Mr McBee?" asked Miss Merriweather in her new, sad, quiet voice.

"I thought you might like to know," said Mr McBee, "that there's a lion. In the library."

Miss Merriweather jumped up from her chair and ran down the hall.

Mr McBee smiled. "No running!" he called after her.

Miss Merriweather didn't listen.

Sometimes there was
a good reason to break the rules.
Even in the library.

WALKER BOOKS is the world's leading
independent publisher of children's books.
Working with the best authors and illustrators
we create books for all ages, from babies
to teenagers – books your child will
grow up with and always remember. So…

FOR THE BEST CHILDREN'S BOOKS,
LOOK FOR THE BEAR